AEA2894

THE LIBRARY OF
CONSTELLATIONS™

Orion

Stephanie True Peters

The Rosen Publishing Group's
PowerKids Press™
New York

For Jackson, my not-so-little guy

Published in 2003 by The Rosen Publishing Group, Inc.
29 East 21st Street, New York, NY 10010

First Edition

Editor: Jannell Khu
Book Design: Michael Caroleo, Michael de Guzman, Michael Donnellan
Photo Credits: Cover, pp. 4, 15, 16, 19 © Roger Ressmeyer/CORBIS; back cover and p. 1 Bode's Uranographia, 1801, courtesy of the Science, Industry & Business Library, the New York Public Library, Astor, Lenox and Tilden Foundations; pp. 6, 7 © Stapleton Collection/CORBIS; p. 8 © Gustavo Tomsich/CORBIS; p. 11 Bill Schoening/NOAO/AURA/NSF; p. 12 © T.A. Rector/NOAO/AURA/NSF; p. 20 digital illustration by Michael Donnellan.

Peters, Stephanie True, 1965–
Orion / Stephanie True Peters.— 1st ed.
p. cm. — (The library of constellations)
Includes bibliographical references and index.
Summary: Discusses the constellation Orion, its location, and various myths about it in different civilizations.
ISBN 0-8239-6164-8 (library binding)
1. Orion (Constellation)—Juvenile literature. [1. Orion (Constellation)] I. Title.
QB802 .P47 2003
523.8—dc21

2001004454

Manufactured in the United States of America

Contents

1 The Winter Constellation   5

2 The Greek Myth   6

3 The Man in the Stars   9

4 A Star Is Born   10

5 Orion's Nebulae   13

6 Star Colors   14

7 Star Sizes   17

8 Rigel, the Double Star   18

9 Betelgeuse, the Variable Star   21

10 The Hunter Points the Way   22

   Glossary   23

   Index   24

   Web Sites   24

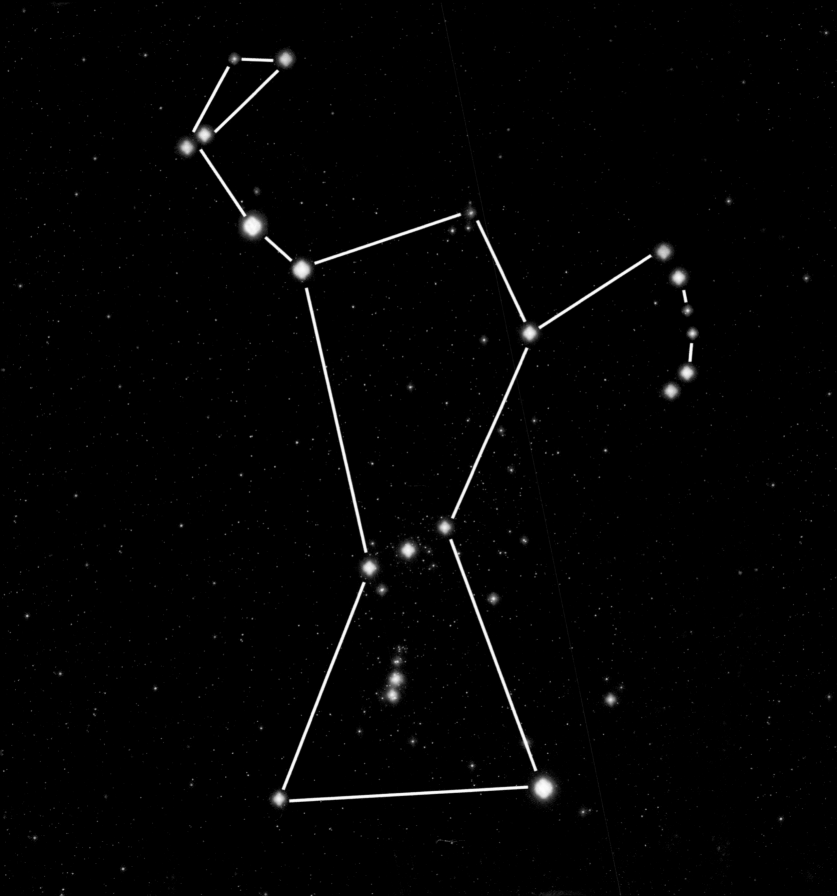

The Winter Constellation

The constellation Orion is also called the Hunter. In the **Northern Hemisphere** Orion lights up the night sky from late fall to early spring. It is easiest to see Orion during the winter, when it is the brightest constellation in the night sky. A constellation is a group of stars that looks like a figure or a shape. Constellations are usually named for people from myths, or for animals and objects. Orion can be seen from almost anywhere in the world.

To find Orion, first look for three bright stars in a row, high in the southern sky. These stars form Orion's belt. Around the belt are four stars that make up a slanted rectangle. Two of these stars represent Orion's arms and the other two stars make up his feet. The column of fainter stars below the belt forms a sword or a **scabbard**. The positions of the stars above his right shoulder make it look as if his arm is raised and is holding a club. Three stars above his shoulders mark Orion's head. A group of stars to the right of Orion's body looks like a shield.

If you connect the star formation that makes up Orion, you can see an outline of a man.

The Greek Myth

There is a well-known, ancient Greek story about the constellation Orion. The ancient Greeks believed Orion was a mighty hunter who fell in love with Artemis, the goddess of the hunt. Apollo, Artemis's brother, did not want Orion to marry her. Apollo tricked his sister into shooting an arrow at a man swimming in the sea. Apollo told Artemis that the person was a criminal, but it was actually Orion! Artemis shot and killed Orion. When she realized what she had done, she begged the gods to bring Orion back to life. Although the gods refused, they allowed Artemis to place Orion in the night sky. A different version of the story tells that Orion was killed by a scorpion's sting. Asclepius, the god of healing, placed Orion in the sky. Even there, he is not safe. Scorpius, the scorpion constellation, follows him across the sky every year. As Orion disappears below the **horizon** each spring, Scorpius comes into view above the horizon.

The ancient Greeks believed Orion was a great hunter. They have stories to explain how Orion became a part of the night sky.

Conomic uouso a th

The Man in the Stars

People have told stories about Orion for centuries. The ancient **Sumerians** worshiped the constellation. The Sumerians were a group of people who established one of the world's earliest civilizations in about 4000 B.C. The Sumerians called this star formation *Uru-anna*, which means the "light of Heaven." The ancient Egyptians, who lived more than 4,500 years ago, knew the constellation as Sahu, a terrible god who hunted other gods and men. The **Hittites**, who lived during the time of the ancient Egyptians, called the star formation Aqhat. They believed Aqhat was killed when another hunter tried to steal his bow. In the Jewish tradition, Orion was thought to be a symbol of a king named Nimrod. The Bible tells the story of Nimrod, who ruled a land called Shinar in **Mesopotamia**. When Nimrod decided he was as powerful as God, he began to build the Tower of Babel to climb to heaven. This angered God. As punishment, God placed Nimrod in the sky. Nimrod was doomed to wander through the heavens forever.

This fourteenth-century artwork shows the story of people building the Tower of Babel.

A Star Is Born

Orion, the Hunter, never actually lived. He is an imaginary character in a story. However, the stars that form the constellation Orion really do have lives. All stars are born. They live and they die. A star is born in a cloud of dust and gas called a **nebula**. Stars are made of **hydrogen**, the lightest gas in the universe. **Gravity**, the force that draws objects together, pulls together hydrogen and tiny **particles** of dust. The gas and the dust form the star's **core**, or center. As the force of gravity packs more dust and gas together in the core, the core begins to heat up. As the core gets hot, it begins to glow. At first it is a dull red color, but it grows brighter in time. This is how stars are born!

Fun Facts

Did you know that the Sun is a star? All stars have ages, as we do. The Sun has lived half of its life, so we can say that it is middle-aged! Many scientists believe that the Sun will live for 5 billion more years.

This star is part of Orion. It glows because it is very hot. Over time stars get hotter and hotter until they slowly start to cool off and change color once again.

Orion's Nebulae

There are two famous nebulae in the constellation Orion. One is called the Horsehead Nebula because it looks like the head of a horse. It is a **dark nebula.** It looks like a dark cloud outlined by the light of the stars around and behind it. The Horsehead Nebula is found below the left star of Orion's belt. The middle star of Orion's sword is the Great Orion Nebula. It looks like a cloud of green mist in the shape of a bat. It is an **emission nebula**, a cloud of dust and gas that is so hot it glows like a lightbulb. Both nebulae are difficult to see with the naked eye. **Astronomers** use strong **binoculars** and **telescopes** to observe them.

Fun Facts

In the spring of 2000, the Hubble Heritage Project asked visitors to their Web site for suggestions as to what picture the Hubble Space Telescope should take. More than 5,000 voters participated, and the clear winner was the Horsehead Nebula! The Hubble Space Telescope is a powerful telescope that orbits in space.

The Horsehead Nebula is the easiest nebula to identify. It gets its name from its resemblance to a horse's head.

Star Colors

When you look at the night sky, all the stars seem to be the same color, but they are not. Powerful telescopes help astronomers see stars that are red, yellow, white, or blue. The color of a star is based on how hot it is. This is similar to how metal changes color when it is heated. For example, when metalworkers heat a piece of metal over a very hot fire, first the metal glows red. As it gets hotter, it turns yellow. As it gets hotter still, the metal looks white. At its hottest, the metal looks blue. It is the same for stars. The hottest stars are white and blue. The cooler ones are red and yellow. The constellation Orion has both cool and hot stars.

A star's color can give us an idea of how old it is. As stars age, they get hotter and change color from red to yellow, then to white, and, finally, to blue. After billions of years, they grow cooler, changing color again as they die.

Powerful telescopes, like this one, help astronomers to see the different colors of the stars.

Betelgeuse

Rigel

Star Sizes

Stars come in different sizes. The smallest stars are called **dwarf stars**. Large stars are called **giant stars**. The biggest stars are known as **supergiants**. They are the superstars of the universe. Astronomers sort stars by color and size. A small, cool star is a red dwarf. A white supergiant, on the other hand, is very big and very hot. Our Sun is a yellow giant. Its size and color fall somewhere in the middle of the scale. Orion is the home of two well-known supergiants. These huge stars are named Rigel, a blue supergiant, and Betelgeuse, a red supergiant.

Fun Facts

Bigger stars burn at a faster rate than do smaller stars. This means they have a shorter lifespan than do smaller stars. Betelgeuse is pronounced beetle juice!

Orion has more bright stars than does any other constellation. The big bright stars Rigel and Betelgeuse help to make Orion stand out in the night sky.

Rigel, the Double Star

Rigel is the seventh-brightest star in the sky. Its name means "left foot of the giant" in Arabic. Rigel can be found below and to the right of the three stars that form Orion's belt. Rigel is a double star. A double star is actually two stars that circle each other around a common center, like both ends of a twirling stick. Rigel is made up of two stars. They are called Rigel A and Rigel B. Rigel A is much larger than Rigel B. In fact you usually need a telescope to see Rigel B. If you had a telescope, you would see that Rigel B is actually a double star itself. Together Rigel A and Rigel B form one very large, bright star. It is 50 times larger and gives off more than 50,000 times more energy than does our Sun.

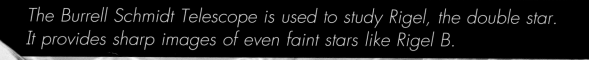

The Burrell Schmidt Telescope is used to study Rigel, the double star. It provides sharp images of even faint stars like Rigel B.

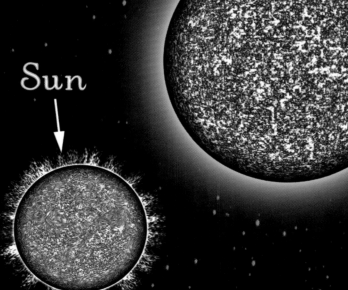

Betelgeuse
(920 times larger than the sun)

Betelgeuse
(500 times larger than the sun)

Sun

Betelgeuse, the Variable Star

Betelgeuse means "armpit of the central one" in Arabic. It is also known as "the shoulder of the giant," which describes where the star is located in the constellation. Betelgeuse marks Orion's right shoulder. It is the eleventh-brightest star in the sky.

Betelgeuse is a **variable star**. Variable stars dim and brighten. They grow and shrink in regular cycles in the course of hours, days, weeks, or years. Betelgeuse gets bigger and brighter as its core heats up. When its core cools down, it shrinks and dims. Betelgeuse's cycle lasts for six years. At its largest and brightest, it is 920 times bigger than the Sun and gives off 14,000 times more energy than does the Sun. Even at its smallest, it is 500 times bigger than the Sun and shines twice as brightly as the Sun.

At the end of its lifespan, a smaller star will meet a quiet end. A bigger star, like Betelgeuse, will die with a huge explosion!

The Hunter Points the Way

When Orion hunts in the night sky, he is surrounded by other wintertime constellations. Once you have found the Hunter, you can find these other constellations easily. Taurus, the Bull, is a *V*-shaped formation that rests on its side above Orion's shield. Above Betelgeuse, positioned on Orion's shoulder, are Castor and Pollux, two bright stars that are part of the constellation known as Gemini, or the Twins. To the left of Betelgeuse is Canis Minor, the Little Dog. Follow Orion's belt downward and you will come to Sirius, the brightest star in the sky and part of Canis Major, the Big Dog. With so much to see in the winter night sky, it is worth bundling up to go stargazing!

Fun Facts

If Betelgeuse were to die and to explode today, it would look like the crescent Moon from Earth. It would cast shadows on Earth, and you would be able to see it during the day!

Glossary

astronomers (uh-STRAH-nuh-merz) People who study the Sun, the Moon, the planets, and the stars.

binoculars (bi-NAH-kyu-lars) An instrument that has two eyepieces and lenses and that magnifies objects.

core (KOR) The center of a star.

dark nebula (DARK NEH-byuh-luh) A cloud of dust and gas outlined by starlight.

dwarf stars (DWARF STARZ) Small, faint stars.

emission nebula (ee-MIH-shun NEH-byuh-luh) A cloud of dust and gas that gives off the light of nearby stars.

giant stars (JY-int STARZ) Very bright, large stars.

gravity (GRA-vih-tee) The natural force that draws objects toward one another.

Hittites (HIT-yts) The people of an ancient civilization of the Middle East.

horizon (her-EYE-zun) A line where the sky seems to meet Earth.

hydrogen (HY-droh-jen) The lightest-weighing gas in the universe.

Mesopotamia (mes-oh-poh-TAY-mee-uh) The ancient name for the land between the Tigris and Euphrates Rivers.

nebula (NEH-byuh-luh) A cloud of dust and gas, the birthplace of stars. The plural of nebula is nebulae.

Northern Hemisphere (NOR-thern HEH-mis-feer) The northern half of Earth's surface.

particles (PAHR-tih-kulz) Very small parts of a larger object.

scabbard (SKAH-berd) A case for a dagger or a sword.

Sumerians (soo-MEHR-ee-ens) One of the earliest civilizations of the ancient world and a part of Babylonia.

supergiants (SOO-per-jy-ints) The brightest, biggest stars.

telescopes (TEH-leh-skohps) Instruments used to make distant objects appear closer.

variable star (VAIR-ee-uh-bul STAR) A star that changes brightness.

Index

A
Apollo, 6
Artemis, 6

B
Betelgeuse, 17, 21, 22

C
color, 14

D
double star, 18

E
Egyptians, 9

G
gravity, 10
Great Orion Nebula, 13
Greek(s), 6

H
Hittites, 9
Horsehead Nebula, 13
Hunter, the, 5, 10, 22

M
Mesopotamia, 9
myth(s), 5

N
nebula(e), 10, 13
Nimrod, 9

O
Orion's belt, 5, 18

R
Rigel, 17, 18

S
Sumerians, 9
Sun, 17, 18, 21

T
telescopes, 13, 14

V
variable star, 21

Web Sites

To learn more about constellations and Orion, check out these Web sites:
http://hubble.gsfc.nasa.gov
www.EnchantedLearning.com/subjects/astronomy
www.lhs.berkeley.edu/starclock